The Friendship Heart

The Friendship Heart

SCHOLASTIC INC.

New York   Toronto   London   Auckland   Sydney

Mexico City   New Delhi   Hong Kong   Buenos Aires

ISBN-13: 978-0-545-02923-0
ISBN -10: 0-545-02923-6

www.onlyheartsclub.com

12 11 10 9 8 7 6 5 4 3 2 1   8 9 10/0

Printed in China
First printing, January 2008

The Only Hearts Girls™ formed the Only Hearts Club® in a bond of true friendship. They are a fun-loving bunch of friends who are always there for one another. They laugh, share secrets, and have the greatest adventures together. Most important, they encourage one another to listen to their hearts and to do the right thing.

*T*aylor Angelique was excited. Her five best friends were coming over for a sleepover. This wasn't just any sleepover though; it was a special one that marked the anniversary of the Only Hearts Club. It was exactly a year ago that the six girls had pledged to always listen to their hearts and to do the right thing.

"They're here!" Taylor exclaimed at the sound of the doorbell. Her beagle, Patches, barked happily, excited to find out who was at the door.

The Friendship Heart

When Taylor opened the door, she smiled at all of her friends standing there.

"So are you going to invite us in, or are we having the sleepover on your porch?" teased Briana Joy.

"Oops! Sorry!" Taylor said with a giggle. "Come on in!"

Later that night, over pizza and soda, the girls talked about all the fun things that had happened in the last year. They had had their ups and downs, but they all agreed on one thing — the Only Hearts Club had helped them be true to their hearts and make the right decisions in the end.

Olivia Hope raised her cup in the air. "I'd like to make a toast: to the Only Hearts Club."

The other girls raised their cups, too. "To the Only Hearts Club!" they cried.

"Hey! You know what we should do?" asked Karina Grace

"Eat more pizza?" joked Anna Sophia.

"Well, besides that," Karina said with a smile as the othe girls laughed. "We should get something to show that we're th Only Hearts Club. Something that only the six of us wil have."

"That's a great idea!" said Lily.

"Yeah, that'd be cool," agreed Briana. "But what should i be?"

The girls thought hard. Olivia suggested matching T-shirts Anna mentioned hats.

Finally, Taylor had a suggestion. "How about friendshij necklaces?"

All the girls broke out into big grins. "That's it! That' perfect!" they cried.

The Friendship Heart

To raise money for the friendship necklaces, the girls decided to have a bake sale. Early the following Saturday, they met at Anna's house. Anna loved to bake and cook; doing it with friends was just the icing on the cake.

"What are we making?" Karina asked.

"I've been looking over some of my favorite recipes and found a few super yummy treats," said Anna. "How about Triple Fudge Brownies and Jumble Surprise Cookies?"

"What's the surprise?" Olivia asked.

Anna smiled. "How good they taste," she replied with a wink. "Now let's get to work!"

Anna's mom helped the girls get set up and turned on the oven for them. Taylor greased the pans, Karina measured out all the ingredients for the brownies, and Olivia mixed everything together and poured the brownie batter into the baking pans.

Meanwhile, Briana, Anna, and Lily worked on the Jumble Surprise Cookies. Anna's cocker spaniel, Bubulina, paced at the girls' feet, hoping some food might accidentally fall to the floor.

As soon as the brownies were ready, Anna's mother took them out of the oven and put the cookies inside. When the girls saw the mouthwatering brownies, they couldn't resist having a little taste.

"We'll just take the six smallest brownies," said Anna.

"I like that idea!" cried Briana, taking her brownie. "Yum! Eating is definitely the best part of baking!"

Anna smiled. "Let's hope the people that come to our bake sale feel the same way!"

The Friendship Heart

That afternoon, the girls packed up their treats and brought them to the park. They spread out a tablecloth on a picnic table and arranged the cookies and brownies.

"Now all we need are some hungry people," said Karina. The girls had hung signs all around the park but they were still worried no one would come to their bake sale.

Before long, word had spread throughout the park about the girls' delicious desserts, and people were gathered around the picnic table. The Jumble Surprise Cookies were bestsellers.

"I told you so!" Anna said with a laugh.

Soon everything was gone!

Taylor counted the money and put it in a small tin. "There's more than enough here to buy us all necklaces," she told the others.

Everyone cheered. The bake sale was a huge success! Taylor volunteered to take the money tin home with her for safekeeping.

The Friendship Heart

As Taylor rode home on her bike she passed the Furry Friends Animal Shelter. Even though she had promised her friends she'd go straight home with the money, she could never resist a chance to play with puppies and kittens. *I'll just stop in for a quick visit*, she thought.

Taylor walked her bike up to the building and leaned it against the bike rack. She felt a little guilty, but the thought of all those cute furry animals distracted her as she opened the door to the shelter.

Suddenly, a little brown shape shot out like a rocket down the sidewalk from the shelter.

"Stop that dog!" called Nikki, the shelter manager.

With no time to lose, Taylor sprinted down the block after the runaway puppy. As she did, her backpack came open, and the money tin fell out.

"Oh, no!" gasped Taylor as the money tin rolled off the sidewalk toward the sewer drain. At that moment Taylor knew she had to make a split-second decision: go after the money, or go after the puppy.

The Friendship Heart

Taylor listened to her heart and dove on top of the puppy.

She had stopped him from running away! The puppy sweetly licked her face, but Taylor's happiness vanished as she watched the money tin disappear down the drain and into the sewer.

"It's a good thing you're cute," Taylor told the puppy as she carried him back to the shelter, "because you're certainly a troublemaker!"

Nikki was waiting for Taylor outside the shelter. "Thank you so much for bringing him back, Taylor!" she said gratefully.

"You're welcome," replied Taylor. "I'm always happy to help."

Taylor was sad as she climbed on her bike and pedaled home. Deep down in her heart she knew that going after the puppy instead of the money was the right decision, but she was really worried. *That money was MY responsibility,* she thought. *How am I going to tell the others that I lost it?*

The Friendship Heart

The following morning, all Taylor could think about was the bake sale money. She was replaying the scene in her mind for the zillionth time when the telephone rang.

"It's Anna for you," Taylor's mother called.

"Thanks Mom," Taylor replied as she nervously picked up the phone.

"Hi T," said Anna. "What are you doing today? Want to go shopping for the necklaces?"

Taylor panicked. "I don't think I can go today," Taylor told her, faking a cough and sneeze. "I'm really sick."

"Well, we're not going without you," Anna said. "You stay home and take care of yourself. We can go shopping next weekend."

"Thanks for understanding," Taylor said.

Phew! Taylor felt a little guilty about lying to her friend, but at least she avoided having to admit that she lost the money . . . for now.

The Friendship Heart

Meanwhile, Anna was busy planning "Operation Get Well." Soon Anna, Olivia, Lily, Briana, and Karina had gathered on Taylor's front porch.

"Taylor!" Taylor's mother called to her, "your friends are here to see you."

"Tell them I'll be right down!" Taylor yelled frantically. Faster than lightning, she threw on pajamas, swiped some of her mom's blush on her nose to make it look red, put a blanket over her shoulders, and ran downstairs to the front door.

"We heard you were sick, so we brought you a get-well care package!" Lily said.

"Can we come in?" asked Olivia suspiciously.

"NO!" exclaimed Taylor. "I mean . . . um, you shouldn't — you might get sick, too. *Cough, cough.* Thanks for all this stuff. See you guys later." Taylor grabbed the bag from Karina and shut the door on her confused friends.

"That was a close one," Taylor said out loud to herself. She should have felt relieved, but instead she felt sad. She hated lying, especially to her best friends!

The Friendship Heart

The next week the hollow ache in Taylor's heart grew. She was so scared to tell her friends about losing the money for the necklaces that she avoided them whenever she could. And the rest of the Only Hearts Girls were starting to notice.

Lily, Karina, and Anna were walking home from school.

"What's up with Taylor?" Lily asked. "Is it just me, or has she been acting really strange lately?"

The rest of the girls agreed.

"Yeah, it's like she's been avoiding us ever since we had our bake sale," replied Karina.

Suddenly, a terrible thought occurred to Anna. "What if Taylor doesn't want to be in the Only Hearts Club anymore!" The girls all gasped.

"That's serious stuff you guys," said Lily. "And I feel weird talking about Taylor behind her back." The other girls agreed. The Only Hearts Club needed to call an emergency meeting — they had to get to the bottom of all this Taylor trouble.

The Friendship Heart

That Saturday, the girls met at the dog park under their favorite tree. Taylor was feeling nervous. She was certain that a special meeting of the Only Hearts Club could only mean one thing — that her friends knew she had lost the bake sale money. Normally Taylor would be laughing and having a great time sitting in the warm sun with her best friends, watching their dogs all frolic with each other. But today it made Taylor feel guiltier.

"Let's call this special meeting of the Only Hearts Club to order," said Anna seriously.

"Yeah," said Briana. "Let's start with Taylor. T, is there anything you want to tell us?"

The heaviness in Taylor's heart was too much to bear. She knew it was finally time to tell the truth. *It's now or never,* she thought. *They already know anyway.*

The Friendship Heart

Taylor took a deep breath. "I lost the money from the bake sale," she blurted out.

Instantly, she felt like a weight had been lifted off of her, and she went on with her confession.

"After the bake sale, I knew I shouldn't, but I stopped at the animal shelter on my way home. Suddenly, a puppy escaped from the shelter. I chased after it down the street, but my backpack came open, and the money tin fell out! It was rolling toward the sewer, and I could have gone after it — but the puppy was running away, so I went after the puppy instead. The money went down the sewer drain, and now it's gone forever." Taylor stopped to catch her breath. "I'm so sorry," she said softly.

The Friendship Heart

Taylor looked at her best friends. "Can you ever forgive me?" she asked in a small voice.

Suddenly, Taylor's friends started to laugh.

"T, we thought you were going to tell us that you didn't want to be in the Only Hearts Club anymore!" exclaimed Anna.

"Why would you think that?" Taylor asked in disbelief.

"Because you've been avoiding us all week!" said Briana.

"And that whole sick act — we knew you were just faking it!" Lily chimed in.

"I'm sorry about that," Taylor said sheepishly. "But what about the money? Aren't you mad at me?"

Karina shook her head. "Well . . . it would have been better if you *hadn't* lost all the money," she said with a laugh, "but accidents do happen."

Olivia agreed. "Besides, by going after the dog, you listened to your heart. . . ."

"And listening to your heart is the most important part of being in the Only Hearts Club!" Briana pointed out.

The Friendship Heart

Taylor grinned. Telling the truth had felt terrific, but the best part was that her friends weren't even mad at her!

The girls left the dog park and decided to visit the animal shelter to meet the runaway puppy. They tied their dogs outside the shelter and went inside.

"I'm afraid you're too late," Nikki told them. "The dog has been adopted by a couple. They were coming to pick him up the day he tried to escape."

"Oh," said Taylor, disappointed. Then she brightened. "Well, at least he's found people to love him."

"And chase after him!" Anna added with a laugh.

Nikki smiled. "I'm glad you came by, Taylor, because the couple left something for you." She handed Taylor an envelope. When Taylor opened it and saw what was inside, her eyes grew wide.

"It's a reward for your rescue," explained Nikki.

"This is awesome!" Taylor exclaimed as she counted the money. "I know just what to do with it!"

The Friendship Heart

At the mall, the girls looked excitedly at necklaces. Olivia found one with a horseshoe charm. Karina found one with a musical note.

"I found the perfect one!" Taylor suddenly exclaimed.

All the girls rushed over to look at the necklace in Taylor's hand. Dangling from the chain was a colorful heart. They all agreed that it was perfect.

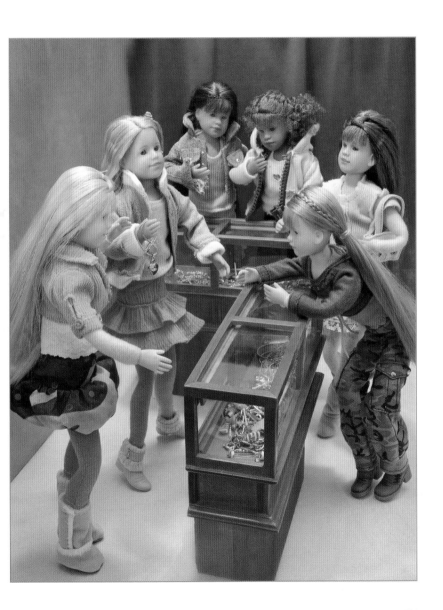

The Friendship Heart

"We'll take six of them, please," Taylor told the salesperson, "for me and my very best friends."

"Now we'll have something to remind us to listen to our hearts," said Lily.

Taylor looked at her friends and smiled. "And if we forget, we'll always have each other to make us remember!"

About the Only Hearts Club

Only Hearts Club® is a fashion doll brand that delivers a positive image and message to girls. The soft, poseable dolls feature amazing detail, and look and dress like real girls, in age-appropriate fashions. The brand's message, delivered through a series of Only Hearts Club books, is to "listen to your heart and do the right thing." This image and message are unique.

As detailed in their books, and through available playsets, outfits, and accessories, the Only Hearts Girls™ share the interests and experiences of real girls. They love horses and enjoy visiting the stable and horseback riding as part of the Horse & Pony Club™.